IMPLUSIVE EMOTION

LOVE COME DOWN

AUBREE PYNN

UNTITLED

Who am I?

I'll be whatever you say

But right now, I'm the sight-raped hunter

Blindly pursuing you as my prey

- Brother of the Night (A Blues for Nina)

1

KENDRA MACKIE

Most of my things were sitting in the middle of Micah's living room. There were still a few trivial things in my car, but they could stay there until I moved into my place in two weeks. My hands rested on my hips as I looked over my things just sitting here in front of me. They looked just as sad as I did. Pitiful leather bags, morbid rolling suitcases, and my least favorite, somber totes full of things I thought would make me happy.

I could have sworn I told myself not to ever end up in a situation, where I depended on a man for anything. Somehow between me telling myself that, pacing the floor with affirmations and being everything to myself, I got sucked inside the vortex of him. He was suave, chocolate, and could talk any woman out of their panties. As charming as it was before, it deemed itself to be an issue later on. A bigger issue than I was willing to deal with. Something about sharing my man wasn't something that I found interest in. Had the shoe been on the other foot, he would have knocked my head clean off of my shoulders for even thinking about another man let alone looking at him. But those rules didn't apply to men.

It was disgusting.

"Kendra, he's calling me now," Micah spoke up, entering her living room. She stopped briefly and looked at all my things and then at me.

"Don't look at me like that Mimi, I'll be out of here in two weeks," I replied, finding the strength to carry a few duffle bags into her guest room.

Micah was on my heels with another set of bags. "How did your crazy ex get my number?"

I pushed my curls out my face and huffed. "Girl, I don't know. You said it yourself. The man is crazy. How does he get locations and back information? It is all beyond me."

"Has to be, to let you get away from him because he couldn't keep his dick in his pants," her rebuttal was fueled with so much detest for him.

I couldn't blame her. I had to confess that she told me not to even go there with him. She told me that I should have kept it professional. She was right. What hurt more than the betrayal, was the fact that Micah was right.

I muttered to myself, "Or his hands."

She was going to gloat in this victory as long as she could. "I'm not going to say I told you so, but I told you so."

"Thank you for the encouragement."

"No, try thank you for getting me that hell out of that house."

Gary and I had broken up months ago, but the lease was in my name, and I refused to break it and ruin my credit. Somehow, he thought that because I was there that he could hang around too. But two weeks after breaking up, he decided that it wasn't his responsibility to cover the bills anymore. Not only that, he had different women in and out but managed to pop up anytime a man was too close to me.

He was really out of his mind. I was so upset with myself for not seeing the signs before I decided to move in with him.

"Thank you," I simply said.

Sitting down on the edge of the queen-sized bed, I placed my head in my hands and sighed. "I have so much to do."

"You do. Don't you have an event tomorrow night?"

I nodded my head and fell back into the pillows. "I do. Twenty people, nothing too big."

"And what are you doing for Thanksgiving?"

I huffed again and rolled my eyes at the thought. "Gavin and Moriah are still roaming around Africa. I'm hoping that I get a last-minute booking, so I could think about feeding people instead of being alone on my favorite holiday."

"Thanksgiving would be your favorite holiday," she said before she snickered.

"Don't do me. You know I like to eat!"

"We all know you like to eat."

I rolled my eyes and threw a pillow at her.

"See, I should have left your ass on the street," she returned, launching the pillow back at me. "Why don't you come to Texas with me? You know my parents do it up, baby."

I loved Micah's parents; they were so warm and loving, but I wanted my parents. I hadn't seen them in months, and I wasn't feeling the idea of having to be up under other people, when I was supposed to be with the family of my own.

My face frowned without me being able to control it. "I don't know, Micah. I don't want to intrude."

She smacked her lips. "I wasn't really asking you. I already told them you were coming."

If looks could have killed, this bitch would have been sprawled out across the floor, lifeless.

"Micah," I groaned. "Why would you get their hopes up like that? You know that they love me more than you."

"Girl, shut up," she forced. "You know damn well that's not the case."

I laughed softly and sat up.

"If my schedule is clear, I'll go."

"Good! Now get your hefty ass up and get the rest of your stuff out my living room."

I was going to end up tranquilizing her. Micah was too much all the time. She didn't come with an off switch. That's why I love her, but the same thing I loved about her was the same shit that drove me crazy.

Now that she was gone, I had a moment of silence to reflect on all the poor decisions I made over the last year. Gary being at the top of the list. Love given, love unreturned, and love wasted. What a fucking waste of love.

Picking up my phone, I hit my recent played playlist and let Jhene's voice fill the room.

Put that on my life, everything I love

Never crossed no line

It was all because I dedicate my life

To lovin' you right

Love comes before pride, I loved you before I

Fore I even knew why

2

DeAndre Yates

"Alright, y'all need to go get your asses home
and rest up because next week. Next week is
the week the world sees what you're made of.
They think we're going to get to Dallas and lose. I don't
want to hear no stories about y'all, and I'm not bailing
you out of jail if you get caught up in some bullshit.
Your ass is going to sit there until we get back." Coach
went on his same rant he bellowed before every major
game.

Once he turned the corner about jail, sex, and drugs, I
tuned his ass out. I was more focused on seeing my
family this year.

My parents didn't miss any details when it came to down to any of the holidays. Since I was playing the Thanksgiving game in our hometown this year, it made getting together a little easier. I was excited to kick it with Ma and Pops. I needed their energy. After being on the road or away from them most of the season, I loved being around them to get centered again.

I stood to my feet and grabbed my leather duffle bag off the shelf of my locker. I was ready to get going. Staying in Arizona another second was bound to drive me crazy. The season had been more than trying, and I needed this week before game day to get my mind right.

As I slung the last of my things over my shoulder, Jermel shouted my name. I groaned to myself, knowing that my quick escape out this locker room just got longer. I had nothing against him. He was a hell of a player, but the nigga could talk. I wasn't in a talking mood. All I really wanted to do was get to my apartment and pack the rest of my things before I flew out to Dallas. My body reluctantly turned around to face him fully. Jermel was standing in front of me with a stupid ass grin on his face. It made me tense up in preparation for whatever he had to say next.

"What you want, fool?" I questioned.

Jermel sucked his teeth and rolled his eyes before going back to his stupid expression. "I just need to know if

Micah is coming to Dallas for the game. I've been DM'ing her and she playing my ass to the side."

He had to be special kind of stupid. "Ay Mel, you know that's my kid sister, right? You really stepping to me and asking me if she's going to be there. Look, we team-mates and all, but you 'bout to cross a line that with me. Slow up."

"Man, I'm just trying to see what's up. I should've kept my mouth shut."

"Yeah you should have," I commented through gritted teeth with my nostrils flared. I turned to walk away from him before I had the urge to victory slap that stupid ass grin off his face. Jermel was a prime example why the league needed to get a better handle on their concussion protocol. He must've taken one too many hits to the head.

My head shook at his nerve as I walked out of the facility and made my way to my pick-up. Micah was about to hear my mouth, whether or not she wanted to. I scrolled through her social media a time or two, she was out here thirst-trapping niggas. I wasn't having too much more of people coming up to me about her.

Shutting my truck door after I climbed my tall body inside; I wasted no time connecting my call from my phone to the car.

"Dre!" Micah sounded off excitedly through the speakers. "Are you on the way?"

"Yeah," I replied with a chuckle. "You excited, ain't it?"

She didn't miss a beat. "Hell yeah! I canceled all my patients for the day. I ain't in the mood to see not another set of teeth."

"Speakin' of teeth. You about to get Jermel's gotdamn teef knocked out his head. Boy, why the nigga thinks it's aight to come up to me talking about you?" I fired off.

She smacked her teeth and huffed. "He so fuckin' thirsty."

"You think your little pictures of your ass is helpin' with that?"

She groaned.

"I'm not responsible for that man's hormones," she defended like I gave a damn.

"You're about to be responsible for fixin' his damn teeth, I know that much. Any damn way. When y'all coming out?"

"Kendra and I are flying out tomorrow. She has one more —"

"Who the hell is Kendra?" I cut her off. "Why you always gotta bring home strays? Every damn year it's somebody else."

"Would your hateful ass shut up," she quipped, accompanied with what I could imagine to be an eye roll. "She's going through some shit and needs a distraction. Don't be mean, please."

"Dre, ain't never mean," I said. "You just got more friends than that nigga from MySpace."

"I swear I am about to hang up on you."

I laughed and asked, "She ain't crazy, is she? Like, I don't need to be locking my shit up?"

"Boy, she ain't studying you. She doesn't even watch football. She's probably going to keep to herself and stay out of the way."

"Good, just how I like it. I didn't sign up for you plus one."

She scoffed. "I should have brought a nigga with me, so you could lose your damn mind. I got to go. Bye, Dre."

Before I check her for that last comment, she hung up.

"That girl is going to make me lose my damn religion," I muttered to myself turning on some Big K.R.I.T and sped up toward my spot. The faster I got there and got my things together, the faster I got to Dallas and relaxed before the Yates crew showed up with this plus one and turned my week upside down.

When I pulled through the gates of my property, I smiled to myself. I was living the dream my parents had for me. It was beautiful and all that shit, but it was fucking lonely. As I climbed out my car, I looked around and smirked. It was painful. I worked hard for all this shit, threw my body into other grown ass men day in and day out and had no one to share this shit with.

Shaking the morbid feeling off of me, I went into the house to try and get some sleep before my parents got there.

"One day."

3

KENDRA

I wasn't one hundred percent sold on this little trip to Dallas with Micah. Already, her mother had sent us a schedule for the week, got extra monogrammed pajamas and a specialty jersey for Thanksgiving Day. I didn't know jack shit about football, and I wasn't about to try and figure it out this week either. When Micah told her brother was in the league, I wasn't the least bit interested. Thirst just didn't run in my veins like that. If I wanted a come up, it was always going to be up to me to provide it.

Dragging my suitcase off the baggage claim ramp; I huffed, blowing the hair out my face. "Why did you let me pack so much?"

"Now how is it my fault that you packed so much?"

I drew my neck back at her and curled my lip up in detest. "Kendra, what if we go out to eat? What if we go swimming, what if we go to a club?"

She scoffed at my reenactment of all her pestering scenarios while I tried to pack in peace just hours ago. "I do not sound like that."

"You do. And I knew better than to pack all this shit." I dragged the suitcase behind me toward the pickup area of the airport.

"Could you cut your whining out for the next seven days, please? I brought you with me, so you could relax. Get your nose out that damn phone and stop thinking about Gary. Seriously, Kendra, fuck him and everything about him. Don't waste your years on fuck boys no more," she started to preach.

I honestly didn't want to hear it. I wasn't worried about Gary; I was worried about how I was going to get more focused on getting my business back on track after letting it fall off. Never again was a man going to get inside my head so bad, to make me feel like I needed to lessen myself to keep him around.

I was going to make it my mission to get back on my shit when I got back to Virginia. I guess for this week, I would allow myself to relax enough to be ready to hit the ground running when I touched down.

"Okay," I simply replied.

"Good, now let's get to this house, pop a bottle, and enjoy a week of no worries."

I nodded in agreeance and followed her to the Uber parked on the curb waiting on us. I took the time to relax and try to catch a nap before Micah had me drunk in a corner somewhere.

Sleep didn't come easy though. It hadn't been easy at all, but I suppose that's what happened when a part of life ends without so much of a warning.

Micah's brother lived almost an hour outside of city limits on a ranch. I was in awe. From the wrought iron entrance, to the curved driveway that gave you a view over acres of greenery, and horses that pranced around to his expansive car collection to the left of the house.

"Damn," I hissed, not having any other words to say.

"It's dope, right? DeAndre is barely here, but it makes for a nice family getaway. Come on," Micah directed, opening her door.

"Ay yo!" I heard a baritone that made a shiver slither down my spine to my center and back up to my brain. "Took y'all long enough to get here."

It was the most beautiful place I'd ever seen in my life. The second the Uber's wheels hit the property; I was hit with an overwhelming sense of peace. It was a feeling like everything that was happening back at home didn't matter at all. My business nothing being what it should have been, or my failed relationship with someone I thought I was going to be with for the rest of my life, didn't matter. Even my parents living their lives on the other side of the planet, didn't matter to me at all. Not here.

I had to give it to this DeAndre guy; he created a haven. It was so warm and welcoming here.

I slid out the blacked-out SUV and tugged at the strap of my duffle bag before making my way to the back of the truck to grab my overpacked suitcase.

"Hey, Dre!" Micah screeched like a banshee as she ran over to her brother and threw her arms around his neck.

I smiled tenderly at their embrace. It almost made me jealous that they had each other. My jealousy quickly faded as my eyes were taking pleasure in how incredibly handsome he was. I should have known though. Micah was beautiful, her parents were breathtaking, but DeAndre. He was a work of art; unlike anything I'd ever seen before.

I was stuck staring at him. I told my eyes to look away, but they refused. They committed every part of him they saw, to memory. From his square cut jaw to the tattoos that wrapped around his thick neck, profoundly cut arms to those massive veiny hands. The tattoos that were placed over his butterscotch skin looked good enough to lick. Shit, this was a bad idea. He was fine and freaking knew it. I could only imagine the hundreds of millions of women that threw themselves at his feet.

He took a few steps in my direction, but I was too lost in the sauce to stop looking at him. His mouth was moving, flashing glimpses of gold and diamonds. My ears heard absolutely nothing that came out of his mouth. All he managed to do was now come into my focus, for me to admire how goddamn beautiful he was. This was the type of man that needed to be posted on a wall, so you could just walk past it and say –

"Damn, lil mama you can't hear me?" his agitated baritone slapped me out of my daydream and back into reality. "Shit, Mimi didn't tell me you were deaf."

My face instantly crinkled up, hearing his comment. "My ears work fine."

"Then why didn't you answer me when I was talking to you just now?" His bushy brows furrowed, almost making his hazel eyes disappear.

Looking up into his freckled face, I groaned. "What was it that you wanted?"

"Well, it sure as hell ain't your little attitude." His country twang had now clashed against my ears. But I still couldn't step back. He was irritating me and making my core suck in all at once.

This had never happened before.

With a roll of my eyes, I returned to pulling my heavy ass suitcase out of the trunk. DeAndre knocked my hand off the suitcase and flashed me a look. "We don't do that 'round here."

"I can take my own bags," I fired back, causing him to scoff; flash his grill again and remove the duffle bag from my shoulder.

"Like I said lil mama, we don't do that 'round here."

I rolled my eyes and huffed before I slowly pulled myself out his presence. It was the most difficult thing I'd ever done. Why the hell was it so hard to get my ass inside of this house? I was so far gone, I looked over my damn shoulder to see if he was watching me walking into the house. He was.

That solidified everything I needed to know. I needed to keep my ass so far away from him for the next seven days. DeAndre should have had a tattoo on his forehead that said, "Warning I'll make you cream your panties within seconds."

Once I got inside, I realized that Micah left me outside to fend for myself. This house was too damn big to be looking for her in every room. I was hoping that he had a housekeeper, or their mom popped out from somewhere to show me around. I was literally standing in the middle of his foyer with my arms wrapped around myself, trying to figure out what the hell life was.

The shiver went down up my spine again. "Micah don't have no damn manners. MICAH!"

I'm not sure if he meant to be so loud, but that roar made my breath get caught in my throat.

"What boy!" Micah shouted back from the top of the stairs.

"How you gon' bring a stray in my shit and just leave her standing down here, looking like she's lost and shit?" he shouted back, starting up the stairs.

"Oh shit, my bad Kendra!" Micah looked over the railing of the stairs at me.

I was shooting DeAndre the meanest mug I could muster up. "Excuse you, I'm not no damn stray."

"Then what are you?" he questioned with his bushy brow raised.

"Leave her alone, Dre. She's good people. Come on Kendra, mom set your room up nice." Micah waved me up the stairs.

Quickly walking past DeAndre carrying all of our bags, I followed Micah to my room for the next seven days. These were going to be the longest seven days of my life. On my way up the stairs, I wanted to push his ass down them and then kiss his boo-boos. This was foreign. This feeling wasn't what I needed. Not right now.

I walked in the room and was even more taken aback by this enormous bedroom. "He can't just play football."

Micah chuckled and DeAndre sounded off again, making me huff.

"I sell drugs too on the side." He sounded close as hell.

Spinning around to see him standing within two feet of me, placing my bags at the foot of the bed. "And I'm a CIA agent."

I rolled my eyes.

"Part time comedian too, huh?" I muttered.

"Yeah, on Sundays. You'll see," he commented with a sexy ass, arrogant ass smirk. "Come on, Micah. I need to light your ass up about Jermel."

"You need to get a handle on your boy. Don't nobody want him."

Micah and DeAndre walked out of the room, leaving me alone. I needed him to get away from me so bad, it was unreal. The second their voices trailed off out of my range, I sighed in relief and dropped my shoulders.

"Thank God."

4

DeAndre

endra was … mine.

Whether it be for the next week or however long.

There wasn't going to be a question about the shit. I knew that from the second she slid her pretty ass out that Uber and tried to walk around to get her bags. I quickly realized that she wasn't used to a man like me, which was going to make this a lot more fun. I had to give it to Micah this time; her choice of holiday stray wasn't all that bad.

I brought my drink to my lips and watched her from the other side of the room. Every night this week, mom had something planned. I didn't mind, especially if I got to study my prey with my feet kicked up.

Micah and Kendra were sitting on the other side of the room with mom, making their signs for the game on Thursday. Kendra was focused on coloring her football with my number in the middle. She laid on her side in a pair of leggings, Victoria Secret hoodie, and fuzzy socks. She was comfortable, enough. But I wanted to see how comfortable she was willing to get with ya boy.

Pops' heavy hand slapped my shoulder as he sat down in the chair. "You ready for Thursday?"

"That ain't a question. I was born ready," I replied, sitting my glass down on the end table and not taking my eyes off Kendra for a second.

She knew I was staring too. She refused to look at me. That was cool though, pretty soon I was going to have her fine ass singing my name like I was her daddy.

"That's what I like to hear," Pops commented.

It didn't matter how many MVP's I had, how many games I played in, he was always going to be my coach. "You ready for the game? Ma told me y'all ain't sitting in the box."

"Hell nah, I ain't sitting in that box with all them damn stuffy ass people. You better pray I don't get my ass on the field."

I chuckled and shook my head. "I don't need you nowhere 'round the field, Pops. I'm going to tell them to keep your ass away from it."

He chuckled lightly and looked at me briefly. He trailed my line of sight to Kendra, who had sat back up and looked at her work.

"I hope I did that right; I don't know the first thing about football," she commented, looking over at Ma.

"Oh, we cannot have that. What do you do on Sundays?" Ma raised her brow and looked at Kendra oddly. "Girl, if I knew you were so far under the rock, I would have pulled you out a long time ago."

"All Kendra does is work," Micah commented and started to clean the mess. "This is the first time in the last twelve hours that she hasn't been on her phone making invoices."

Kendra rolled her alluring golden eyes and stood to her feet. "I got to make money. Speaking of which, I got a few more to send off."

"No, you don't," Micah spoke up.

"Mimi, you aren't about to boss me this week, k?" she fired back.

"Girl, stop the act," Micah snickered. "Send them invoices from right here. We're about to break out the Henny."

Kendra's face frowned. "Who the hell drinks that?"

"What, you can't handle it?" I countered, making her look at me. I smirked and dragged my tongue over my grill.

Kendra let a soft grimace make her eye squint and lip curl. "No, I'd rather keep the hair off my chest and remember what the hell happened."

"Oh, yeah," I said with a chuckle. She turned her back to me and said something to Micah I couldn't make out.

I muttered to myself. "I got some shit you will never forget."

"Alright, let's get the drinks going before grandma Kendra taps out on us," Micah spoke up, walking into the kitchen.

Kendra trailed behind her and said softly, "I am not fucking around with y'all. I'm drinking wine and going to sleep. That's it."

Pops looked at me with a smirk on his face. He already knew what I was thinking. I wasn't even going to act like I wasn't trying to break Kendra off something real.

"Son, beware," he mumbled before he pushed himself out of the chair. "She don't look like nothing to toy with it."

For the rest of the night, I silently watched as she sipped her glass of wine and pecked away on her phone. Occasionally, she would look up and comment on the conversation going on, but moments later she was right back into her phone. All that couldn't have been work. I needed to know if she had a nigga. I mean, I didn't care if she did or she didn't. I wasn't worried about him. All men knew never to let their women go around a man with means for a week.

I would have never let my girl go nowhere without me. For a number of reasons. I didn't need nobody looking at her crazy, talking to her crazy, or thinking they could dive in for the kill, like I was about to do.

Micah was in and out of sleep on one end of the couch and Ma and Pop had turned in for the night.

"Your nigga checked in on you yet?" I asked her.

She continued to peck at her phone for a few more moments before she glanced up from her screen at me. "Nah, I don't need to check in with anyone."

"I forgot. You got it. Hm, it's a damn shame though. Shouldn't no man let you out his sight. As fine as you are." I stood to my feet and stretched. "Micah, wake yo drunk ass up and take ya girl with you."

Kendra groaned and hit Micah with the back of her hand. Micah popped her head up and looked around. "What?"

"What is wrong with him?"

"Girl, don't pay no mind to Dre. He don't get out often."

"Hm," Kendra scoffed. "You might need to give him some manners."

She was irritated; good. I had her right where I wanted her.

5

KENDRA

"Get off the phone, put your onesie on and come on," Micah made herself as clear as humanly possible. So loud, I could hear her through the bathroom door.

"For you to assume that I'm in here on the phone is unfair and I am offended," I responded, securing the towel around my body before opening the door.

"Be offended all you want. I bought you out here to get away from work and Gary, and all you've been doing is working and probably texting Gary." Micah pushed past me and walked into the bathroom, making herself comfortable on the vanity chair.

I loved Micah, but I was starting to realize that intrusiveness ran in the family. For three days, I'd been ducking and dodging DeAndre like my life depended on it. His sly ass comments, staring and his overall presence was getting to me. He had managed to irritate the shit out of me and make want to laugh or drag this ass over his face time after time.

"You don't know what personal space is, do you?" I asked.

She shook her head no. "Not at all. And if I leave you in here alone, I'm going to be waiting on your ass forever."

I shook my head and quickly rubbed lotion over my body before getting into my onesie that Micah and Mrs. Yates insisted that I wore. My ass barely made it inside of it.

"I told you stop eating."

"Bitch, I've been depressed let me live," I replied, smacking my lips.

"I can tell, your ass is getting bigger by the second," Micah said then laughed and walked out the room.

Before I walked out the room in this bright red onesie, I stopped by the mirror to make sure I didn't look as stupid as I felt. My initials sat right over my left breast. I couldn't lie; I filled this thing out nicely. Which could have been a bigger problem than I thought.

DeAndre didn't have to say he was trying to bend me over and get a taste. It was all over his face. I'd been avoiding him, avoiding drinking too much, avoiding eye contact, and avoiding this feeling in the pit of my stomach. DeAndre was one of those men who just had it. He had it and he knew he did. That was probably big dick energy. Energy that if I lost my step for a second, I was going to slip and fall on it.

He was confident and could command a room. That was the shit that would have any woman I knew making breakfast in the morning and serving dessert at the end of the night. Shit, he was the type you gave an attitude to just so he could fuck it out of you.

"Come on!" Micah hollered from down the hall.

Her loud ass pulled me out of my head. With a huff and some silent affirmations, I walked out the room. An affirmation that I had to repeat to myself was that, I was not going to give into DeAndre, I was not going to treat myself and be reminded what good sex could be like. I hadn't had good sex in a minute. In years to be exact.

As I stepped into the game room, Micah shoved a shot of Hennessy into my chest. "Drink up, I need you on one before flip cup."

"I am not playing flip cup with Henny," I whined.

30

"If you scared, baby, just say you scared," DeAndre spoke up from across the room.

DeAndre's comment made my expression drop and look at him with a hint of agitation.

"Would you leave her alone? Damn," Micah spoke up.

Watching them go back and forth, I couldn't help, but stare at him in that white tee that hugged all his muscles and every girl's fall favorite--gray sweatpants. This man was sexy; that was it. I was burning up, and I was crazy to think that this shot of Henny was going to cool me down when I threw it back. My wince was followed by a cough.

"Shit." My whine was mixed with a hiss and a tinge of regret.

DeAndre smirked, looked me up and down, then ran his thick tongue over those full rosewood lips.

Why did he feel the need to keep doing this to me? I didn't have panties on but if I did, they'd be his. I wasn't the type of chick to fuck on my friend's brothers but dammit DeAndre was making this hard. He was making it hard to turn my eyes away as he held my gaze. He was making it hard to breathe. He was making it hard for me to stop having the same vision of him slowly, seductively rolling that huge tongue over every inch of my flesh.

"It goes down smooth, doesn't it?" he finally spoke up, making my eyes flutter and a shiver to pulse through my body. "Now that lil mama got her warmup shot, let's get to it!"

"Now, your mother and I have been doing this long before y'all were born," Mr. Yates spoke up. "Just know y'all about to be on your ass."

I frowned a bit. The ping pong table was set up with ten cups already filled with Henny. I wasn't a Hennessey drinker. Micah was an avid one though, so was the whole family. All I could do was dive in and pray I woke up with all of my dignity and memory intact.

I took my place at the table by Micah and wearily looked at her. She wasn't the least bit concerned about how I felt.

"Aight so listen, lil baby," DeAndre started, throwing his heavy arm over my shoulder. "I'm going to be your partner, so you're not passed out in a corner."

I frowned again, looking up into his eyes. "Listen, I don't need your help."

He chuckled, leaning down to press his lips against my ear. "You need me more than you know, baby. Drink up."

I found enough strength without my melting center, to pull myself out of his control. "That's where you got me wrong, you need me."

I grabbed a cup and took it to the head. "Best of luck to you, though."

From flip cup to bouncing my ass to a UGK mix to get these paper balls out the Kleenex box strapped to my waist.

"Ayyyy!" Micah shouted, holding her cup in the air. "Momma, I think Kendra got you."

"Don't nobody got nothing on my baby!" Mr. Yates spoke up.

Normally, bouncing my ass in mixed company didn't happen. Scratch that; bouncing my ass anywhere didn't happen, but I blamed all of this on the Henny and Micah's drunken cheering. The song was ending in thirty seconds, and I had two more balls left. Mrs. Yates had four, and I couldn't take another shot if I lost to her. I had to bring out my good stuff. From a light twerk, I bust out my full-blown moves to shake that last two balls loose.

"BAM!" I cheered, jumping up and down. "Take y'all shots!"

"I cannot compete with young knees," Mrs. Yates commented as she laughed and pulled me into a hug.

"You'll get me next time. I'm sore and I'm hungry."

"Say less!" Mr. Yates shouted, popping to his feet. "Come on, watching all this ass shake done made me ready to eat something."

From the look he gave his wife, I knew it wasn't food he was hungry for. I wasn't going to stand around to find out what it was either.

I gripped Micah by her wrist and dragged her down to the kitchen with me. I was not going anywhere in the house alone.

"I'm so drunk," Micah giggled before staggering across the kitchen.

I shook my head and rolled my eyes. Funny how the ringleader of drunken antics was too drunk to stand up straight. "Would you sit your drunk ass down somewhere?"

"What are you about to make?" she slurred, looking at me with hooded eyes.

Micah was about ten minutes from becoming a whiny drunk in need of all of my attention. I was tipsy enough to peel this damn onesie off and walk around here without giving a fuck. However, I was nowhere near where Micah and the rest of them were. I learned a long time ago that to have a successful night of drinking, you had to hydrate.

Pulling out the leftovers from dinner, I fixed us a plate and warmed them up in the microwave.

"Damn, can the man that owns the house get something to eat?" DeAndre's loud voice hit my ears. I tossed my head over my shoulder toward the table.

I was too tipsy to try to ward him off with my mouth. I wanted to eat and take my ass to sleep.

"What do you want to eat?" I questioned, giving Micah her plate and going back to the containers.

He didn't miss a beat to stand behind me and pressing his dick against my ass. DeAndre rested his chin on my shoulder and pressed the palm of his hands on the counter, boxing me in. "You."

I stopped breathing, clamping down on my lip. He had to get away from me. I grunted, pushing him back with my ass. "Get away from me. Quickly."

He licked his full lips, snickered and went to sit down at the table with Micah.

6

DeAndre

I was one drink away from being fucked up and being on my ass. Following up with these old heads and Micah. It was clear to me that Micah's minor in college may have been drinking. A degree that she proudly honed as she went through her life. Kendra, on the other hand, had stopped drinking with us, after the second round of losing to me in flip cup.

She couldn't hang, but it was cute that she tried. Matter of fact, it was cute that she walked around my house for the past three days like she didn't see a nigga. She'd been stealing glances on the low, and I was cool with it. It only gave me more motivation to bend her pretty ass over. I wasn't the type of nigga to fall in love quickly, but I was the type to fuck up a mind or two just so I could see how strong-willed they actually were.

A lot of women preached that they wouldn't let a man break them down and have their way. However, a lot of women hadn't ran into the right man to make them cream off of words alone. Something told me that if I let Kendra act on the freaky fantasies she'd been having, I wouldn't regret it. Shit, I highly doubted that she would either. She'd been giving a nigga the eye like I was a piece of steak.

Ma and Pops had already tapped out and staggered to their room after we finished the last game. They were going to have a hell of a hangover in the morning. I made a mental note to be loud as hell when I woke up. Payback was a bitch. All those times they got extra loud when I slept in from partying too hard the night before, was going to come back tenfold.

"Kendraaaa," Micah whined, prancing in the middle of the living room. "Come on, I'm tired."

Kendra laughed softly while lifting the pillows to the couch. "Girl, you're so needy when you get drunk. You can sleep without me. I need to find my phone."

"Ain't nobody calling you on that phone. Come on, I just need you to talk to me until I pass out," Micah continued.

Kendra halted, huffed lightly, and looked over her shoulder at my spoiled drunken sister. "I'll be there in a second. I just need to find my phone."

Micah groaned one last time before huffing up and stomping past me. "You better not leave me hanging."

I laughed to myself as I watched Kendra roll her eyes at Micah. She chewed at the corner of that pretty ass mouth. Every time she laughed or smiled, or licked those juicy ass lips, I wanted to kiss them. And after she got acquainted with my lips, I wanted them wrapped around my dick while she looked up at me with those piercing hazel eyes.

Kendra mumbled something to herself before snapping her fingers and walking up the stairs. My feet took off behind her without much thought. I followed her as she cut the corner to my game room where the party started hours ago. The flashback of her ass bouncing up and down trying to get the balls out the tissue box strapped to her waist, was still fresh in my mind.

Resting my shoulder on the frame of the door, I smirked happily enjoying the view of her round ass bent over searching for her phone under the recliners and ottoman. "You need help, lil mama?"

She jumped slightly as she straightened up. Kendra glanced at me and her eyes danced as she looked me up and down. With her eyes stuck on the print in my sweatpants, her mouth fell open. It took her a few seconds to realize how hard she was staring at a nigga before she pulled her eyes away and cleared her throat.

Kendra squeezed her eyes shut in attempts to collect herself and reset. "I -uh- thought. I thought I left my phone up here."

I scanned over my game room and spotted it on the edge of the pool table. "Is that it?"

The sound of relief escaped her lips as she started across the room for it. This was my time to strike. She had my dick begging for her touch. It was too damn hard to control myself. By the time Kendra spun around--with her nose back in that phone like it had been all week--I was standing there.

"I thought I asked you to stay away from me?" she questioned after she bumped into me and bit that lip again. "Are you going to move?"

I gently removed the phone from her hands and tossed it over the recliners. "I don't know, if you want me to. Do you want me to?"

I licked my lips and dropped my gaze to focus on those eyes that had me spellbound from the second she climbed her pretty ass out the car.

She didn't move. She didn't flinch as I gently traced my pointer and middle finger over her velvety caramel coated skin.

"You got to tell me something, baby?" I spoke up again.

Her eyes traced my lips, the tightness in my jaw, my arms and back down to my pants. This time, she licked her lips before flashing her eyes wearily to the door.

"I can't fuck with you, DeAndre," she finally spoke up.

That wasn't the answer that I wanted, and I knew damn well that that wasn't the answer that she wanted to give me.

"Mm," I rumbled with soft laughter. "Say it again, like you mean it, and I'll fall all the way back."

She stopped fighting her impulse with her control. Reaching her manicured hands out to touch my chin, she bit her lip.

"You and that lip. I'll give you a fucking reason to bite it," I growled lowly in her ear.

I hadn't done shit to her body yet, but Kendra dropped her head back and moaned. "What if somebody walks by?"

A soft kiss to her neck made her breathing hitch. "They sleep. I ain't worried about them. I'm trying to get to know you."

With another kiss to her neck, my hands trailed over her breast that sat up on their own without a bra, and then around her waist; my hands gripped it firmly. When my lips finally connected with hers, her arms draped over my shoulders. I lifted her body up and sat her on the edge of the pool table.

My hands slipped inside her onsite and caressed her breast. My tongue still massaged hers, while her hands found the top of my sweats.

Kendra wasted no time freeing me and pulling away to notice that the sweatpants weren't telling any lies. I was rested fully between her thighs as she held me in her hand. She hesitated.

"Shit," she hissed.

I laughed and placed a hand gently yet firmly at the base of her neck. She couldn't pull her eyes away. For a minute, she had a nigga thinking that his shit was fucked up. Then I saw the flash of hunger in her eyes. Kendra went from frightened to hungry. I swore she slurped up the excess saliva in her mouth.

"Mm," she grunted like she'd been starved. It seemed to me that whatever nigga she had before wasn't feeding her right.

I slowly licked my lips while making my dick jump in her hand.

"DeAndre, you are a beast."

I tightened my grip on her neck, bringing her attention from my rod on her thigh to my face. Her eyes were low and full of lust.

I roughly tongued her down before saying, "I assure you that my mother raised a gentle beast. You trying to find out or leave me hangin'?"

Her legs wrapped around my waist, bringing me in closer and she laid back on the table. She had to still be buzzing from earlier, and I was here for it.

I wasted no time getting her naked and massaging the pink pearl that poked out at me. It was calling me to taste it. One taste of Kendra, and I knew by the way she moaned and melted that this was going to be the best pussy to date.

Her white nails traced my waves, pushing me further into her folds.

"Mm," she hummed against her teeth with her ankles looked around my neck. "Shhhiiiiittttttt."

She wasn't missing a serving of her fruit. Not only was Kendra sexy as hell, she tasted better than sin. I was sure that her shit had me moaning, too. I was definitely smacking my lips like this was my last meal.

Her hands cupped her breast. She was ready for me, if I spent any more time down here, her loud ass moans were going to cause us to have an unwanted audience.

I stood up and fully stepped out of my sweats and pulled that thick ass to the edge of the pool table. "You good?"

She breathlessly answered, "Yes."

Kendra reached down and placed me at her opening. I had to remind myself to pull out. If she felt as good as she tasted, I would get lost in the sauce.

With a loud grunt, I tried to muffle behind my lips. I pushed deeper inside of her walls.

Just like I thought. "You got some good ass pussy, baby."

She had her bottom lip clamped firmly between her teeth, fingers gripping the edge of the table and eyes rolling back into her head. With each stroke, her moans rose higher.

Without further notice, I went from taking it easy on her to trying to fuck her brains out. She sat up wrapping her body around mine and damn near screamed. Covering her mouth with my hand, I kept my stroke until she unraveled, which prompted me to get mine before she woke everybody up.

Kendra pushed me away, slid off the table, and dropped down to her knees. Got damn, lil baby wasn't playing.

Kendra wrapped those lips around my dick, sucked her juices off and bobbed and weaved until I was firing my kids down her throat.

Her tongue traced her lips after I pulled myself out of her mouth. She gathered her clothes and quickly got dressed. As she went to grab her phone, she looked back at me and said, "You should be good now that you got that out of your system."

No, I wasn't good. I watched her walk out of the room and down the hall. The only thing she'd done to my system was managed to make me seek out another opportunity to fuck her again.

7

KENDRA

I tried. I really, really tried not to fuck him. The dick against my ass was the final straw. That was the thing that sent me over the edge. I didn't regret it. I hadn't had sex that good in years. Gary was too busy fucking everything else that when it came down to me and my needs, nothing ever happened. I was tired of getting off on a vibrating mold of a veiny, black dick. I'd been craving a real one and now that I finally got it, I thought I that I was going to be cool.

I was wrong.

I'd been standing in this cold shower, trying to calm my body down. My yoni quivered at the thought of DeAndre. It was absolutely annoying; I hadn't had any sleep all night. I wanted to crawl out of bed and walk my horny ass down to his room and do it again. I knew better. One time was enough anything after that, was going to have me hooked like a crack addict.

At this point, I didn't care that my once silk pressed hair had returned to its natural state. I just wanted to rid myself of the urge to fuck him as the sun came up.

"Kendra, you've done it now, girl," I fussed at myself, turning the water off. "No more Henny for you. No matter how much Micah whines about it."

I dragged my eyes over to the screen of my phone that sat on the edge of the sink. It was seven in the morning, which meant that I was trying to calm my purring kitty down for almost two hours. How sad was this?

I dried off, rubbed some shea butter on my skin, and got dressed in a pair of leggings and long sleeve t-shirt. From the sounds of it, everyone was still sleeping. I had time to make breakfast and go walk around this massive property and see what else he had tucked away.

Jogging lightly down the stairs, I choose to leave my phone in the room. As to be expected, I was floating on a cloud of endorphins. It was beautiful, but I slipped up last night. I had to stay away from him, so he wouldn't break my pussy because all signs led to it.

I'd made myself familiar with his kitchen a few days ago. Making breakfast was easy, the eggs and bacon were on a serving dish along with waffles and fruit. I sat at the table alone and started picking away at my food.

"Hm," I heard him snicker before fully walking into the kitchen. "It was that good that you got up to make breakfast, huh?"

I flashed red. I know I did because my face was burning. "You are so sure of yourself."

"You damn right, I am. Did you sleep good?"

I wasn't about to tell him that the imprint of his dick inside of my walls had me up all night.

"As good as expected."

He winced. "Damn, if it was really good, your ass should have still been knocked out."

"If only my body knew that," I muttered, getting up from the table.

"What you say?"

I shook my head. "Nothing, eat up."

"Where you going?"

"On a walk," I simply replied, trying to get away from him as fast as humanly possible, before my legs were spread open between the bacon and eggs.

He let me slip out of the kitchen with ease, thank God. I went to grab my boots and head out the front door, only to find him leaning against the rail of the front porch.

"Really? Why can't I turn around in a circle in this house without you popping up somewhere?"

He laughed, licked those juicy ass lips, and then smiled warmly at me. "Because for one, it's my damn house. Two, it's you in my damn house. Three, if you walk around this property alone your ass is going to get lost, and I don't have the time to find you."

"I can find my way back."

He nodded slowly. "You want to take a stab at it lil mama, or you wanna walk with me? I know you want to."

"You have no idea what I want."

He stepped to me and closed the gap. "How much you willing to bet on that?"

I gulped loudly, looking into those piercing eyes. DeAndre pressed his soft lips against mine before pulling my bottom lip into his. He sucked on it long enough to make me do whatever he said.

"Let's walk." He stepped back and held his hand out.

I took it because, shit, because I wanted to. We walked from the driveway to the horse stables, to the trail that led to the gazebo in the middle of the pond. I took in the scenery of the sun shining over the dew-coated grass and still water.

"It is so beautiful out here," I said breathlessly, leaning on the rail.

His presence wrapped me up and oddly enough, I was comfortable. Completely comfortable. I sighed, letting everything on my mind go for a while.

"This is one of my favorite spots out here. It's the reason why I bought it."

"What makes someone buy an estate this big as a single man? The women love this, don't they?"

He rumbled with laughter and said, "Nah, ain't never brought nobody out here."

"Boy, run your game on somebody else. I know they trippin' over you," I replied with a laugh and a side eye.

He frowned his face. "I don't run game. I sure as hell ain't out here fucking random women for fun, either. I like my peace."

I turned to face him fully. "I know that comment to be a lie. I'm sure as hell a random woman you fucked on the pool table last night."

He smiled. "Kendra."

My name sounded so good coming off his lips. "Don't even start to feed me no bullshit, Dre. I was with a man who fed me every line in the book. I'm good. It is what it is. I don't need to be your girl or nothing like that. I get it."

"You know all the answers don't you."

"Yeah."

"No, you don't," he responded, looking away from me. "I'm unlike any man you've ever messed with before. I see what I want, and I go get it. Professionally and personally. I knew from the moment your pretty little ass pranced out that car, you were going to be mine."

I laughed and rolled my eyes. "You play games and it's funny. I'm going back to the house."

I turned to walk away, only for him to pull me back into his hard chest. "I'm not done with you yet."

I scoffed. "You're the type that's going to play around with me. I don't have time for it. I've fallen for the wrong man before. I won't —"

He cut me off with a kiss. His tongue invaded my mouth and his arms wrapped around my waist. My efforts were useless. Dre was going to make it a point to turn me out and send me back to Virginia with a broken cootie cat. It was only going to purr for him, and I was going to be out of my mind behind it.

"You won't what?" he quizzed, breaking our kiss to stroke my curly hair out my face. "Won't fall for someone that's gonna wreck your heart again?"

Why was I so damn emotional about this? I wasn't going back to Gary, and I didn't have any feelings towards him other than pure hate. Something about DeAndre looking deep into my eyes and demanding to answer a question, was making my eyes flood.

This was not a love connection. This was sex. Good, mind-numbing sex.

"I can't do that again. That's why I need to stay away from you, but you won't let me."

"Why would I let my future walk away from me?" he asked softly. I felt that shit in the pit of my stomach.

I blindly believed him. Something I knew better than. Four days, and this man had managed to open me up and damn near pour me out.

"You ain't gotta believe shit I'm saying to you. But trust me, you gon feel that shit."

That was the last arrogant comment he made before kissing me, sitting and pulling me down to his lap. My ponytail was gripped and pulled backward, so he could fully access my neck. This sex on impulse was going mess me up. I would have to deal with it later.

His thick fingers found their way inside my leggings. "That's cute, you thought putting on some panties was going to keep you in control."

"Would you shut up?" I groaned, feeling his fingers invade my walls.

"Shut up and what?" His cocky ass smirk was going to make me cream, and I hadn't even gotten the dick yet.

By far, DeAndre had been the only man to make cream and it was so damn good.

I placed my hands on the sides of his face while my hips rotated around his fingers. "Shut up and fuck me."

He smirked and shook his head no. He pulled his fingers out of me and placed them in my mouth while yanking my leggings down with the other. "Nah. That's what you want. You thought, fucking you senseless and walking away is easy. You gon ride this shit and look me in my eyes."

I finished sucking my juices off his fingers and stepped out my leggings. His dick was in his hand; throbbing, dripping, and waiting on me to sit on it. I wanted to. No, I needed to. But before I got to that, I needed to kiss that beautiful, brown dick. Bending over to pull him between my lips, I slurped him up before gliding this pussy down on him.

"Oh shit," he hissed, holding my ass in his hands. "Gotdamn."

My head dropped back as I grinded my hips against him. A hard smack to my ass made me pick my head up and look at him.

"I told you to look at me while you ride this dick. I meant it," he growled. "Don't take your eyes off me."

"You'll fall in love with me if I do," I whined. "You and I both know —"

"Kendraaa," he grunted, dragging out my name. "Don't fucking tell me what I know, baby. Ain't shit I do that's not intentional."

He felt so good, I couldn't fight a thing he said. From the way he was staring into my eyes, I knew he was a goner, and so was I.

After another forty-five minutes of riding, sucking and licking, we pulled ourselves together. "I made a mess all over your sweats."

"Ain't no biggie," he responded, scooping up my panties off the bench.

"I need those."

"Not necessarily. I'll give them back to you tonight."

I frowned and looked at him shove my pink lace panties into his pocket. "What's tonight?"

"Ma and Micah are going to get dragged to the store with Pops to get everything for dinner. You and I are going to chill.

"When you say chill, you mean like regular people without touching and kissing, right?"

He laughed and kissed my lips. "Can't guarantee that I won't kiss and touch you but, I just want to spend some time with you. So, you know I just don't want your body."

"You're mighty forward after four days."

"A man knows what he wants within minutes. But since this is your first time around a real one, I'll break you in easy."

I rolled my eyes. "Whatever you say."

"Whew," he scoffed. "Don't make me make them sexy eyes of yours roll for real."

I chose to walk back to the house before I ending up on his face for a third time in two days.

When we got back to the house, his parents and Micah were in the kitchen chowing down on the breakfast I made before I ended up riding Dre like a stallion.

Micah didn't miss a beat. "Where y'all been?"

"I showed her around the property before she ended up lost somewhere."

"Mmhmm," Micah hummed, looking at me. "Must be windy outside, Kendra your hair is a mess."

"You have the blow dryer and flat iron, nosey," I quipped, nipping the suspicions in the bud. "I'm going to go and try to do my hair, so I don't look like I've been fighting all my life."

"Yeah you do that," Micah quipped back.

I rolled my eyes and started up the stairs. I didn't take long for Dre to follow me and say, "Don't straighten it. I like it like that."

8

DeAndre

"I don't know what that girl is doing," I scoffed, looking at Micah with a twisted face like I didn't have plans of my own with Kendra. I wanted to tease her and tell her that the stray she brought down here, was a few strokes away from me putting her on my insurance.

I had never been the man to fall in love at first sight or anything like that. Women had to prove themselves with me. My ex told me time after time that it felt like I had her in bootcamp to be my woman. I needed to make sure whoever I was with could handle me and everything that came with the life I lived.

Kendra had displayed those traits from the second she got sassy with me. She didn't care about what I did, what I had in the bank, or what I could do for her. Matter of fact, all the avoidance and playing hard to get made me want to pursue her more.

She was right; if I looked into her eyes, I was going to fall, which meant that the door was open for me to catch her.

"Sure, you don't, Dre. You need to leave my friend alone; she didn't come here to get all caught up with you."

"First of all, shut your little ass up. Second of all, I ain't all that bad to get caught up with."

Micah squinted her eyes and looked at me, then she looked me up and down. "Leave her alone. She needs to be relaxing not ducking and dodging you."

There was more Micah wanted to tell me, I could tell. Instead of going any further, she huffed, grabbed her jacket and stomped out the door.

I shook my head and shut the door behind her. "That girl needs a damn hobby."

I walked into the kitchen to pop a bowl of popcorn and grab a bowl of fruit for Kendra. I noticed that when she snacked, she didn't mindlessly do it; it was always fruit or veggies. It was a habit that I thoroughly enjoyed.

Hiking up the stairs, I walked past her room with the door open. "You coming?"

"Yeah, hold on." Her voice was soft.

It made me smile. When she walked out the room in her Virginia State t-shirt and a pair of biker shorts, I smiled wider. "You don't care, do you?"

"About what?" she asked, popping a brow up.

I chuckled and continued to the game room. "You don't care about getting all dolled up."

"For what, we're watching a movie in your house. And if you were alluding to the fact that I don't care about you being a super athlete, the answer is no I don't."

She continued to trail behind and mumbled something she thought I couldn't hear. "And what does it matter? I'll be gone in three days; you'll forget all about me."

If she only knew that I wasn't trying to forget about her. I actually was looking for a way to get her to stay longer. Kendra had a power that she clearly never used for evil or for her sake. Between her eyes, her spirit and her good loving, she could bring an army to its knees or make a man do whatever she said.

We were settled in the recliners in the game room, watching Hobbs and Shaw. She was into the movie, but I was more into her and that comment she made earlier.

It was bothering me. I was trying to hold on to it and not make this night go soft.

I patiently waited until the movie was almost over to look at her and ask, "What did you mean by that earlier?"

"What did I mean by what?" she asked, pulling her eyes away from the screen to me.

"That in three days, I'm going to forget you."

She shrugged and pulled the blanket she had wrapped around her, tighter. "You are. Let's not fool ourselves. This is sex. It's not love. It's not feelings running wild. You saw me and wanted to fuck me. I saw you, and I felt the same way."

I looked away from her and chuckled. "You need to go get your ears checked, lil ma. I'm supposed to be the one who can't hear shit. But you clearly don't be listening to nothing I be sayin'."

"DeAndre, you can't tell me that you want more than this right here and right now."

Kendra was stubborn. It was unbelievable how hard she was trying to talk herself out of the best thing that had ever happened to her. Quite frankly, all I wanted her to do was to give into me, so I could take it from there. This song and dance she was doing was irritating the shit out of me.

I stood to my feet and turned the movie off. "Come here."

She huffed and looked at me with wild eyes.

"Leave your attitude here, or this ain't going to turn out good for you. Come on."

I walked out the game room and down the hall to my bedroom. Kendra walked in slowly behind me and wrapped her arms around herself, as she looked around at the red walls and black furniture.

"Don't be scared now. We done got all that shit out the way," I spoke up. "You know when I first saw you, I wanted to fuck you just to say I did; the second time, I wanted make you unravel, but tonight, I'm going intentionally make you understand that what I want ain't something that's going to end after seven days."

"Dre—"

"Kendra."

I knew she didn't want to get hurt again.

I closed the door and locked it before stepping behind her. My arms wrapped her body, pulling her arms from one another. "You've been hurt. That nigga disrespected the fuck out you."

My hands trailed from her arms up her stomach, over her breast to her neck. Grabbing her neck and her chin and tilting her head back, so she could see my face. "I ain't him. I'm never going to be him or any other nigga that hurt you. I want you to myself."

My kisses to her lips, face, and neck were all passionate. I wanted to wake up to her curled up beside me.

She moaned lightly against my lips. Kendra turned around to let her hands roam over my body. My hands had their way with her. But I was cautious not to go for the kill yet. She removed my clothes, I gladly peeled hers off too.

I stepped back and admired how beautiful she was. Her pretty caramel skin didn't have a blemish in sight.

"Don't look at me like that," she spoke softly and uncomfortable under my gaze.

"Like you're beautiful."

As long as I was fucking her, she didn't mind but when I was standing here taking her in, she squirmed and tried to hide herself from me. That wasn't going to work for me.

"Dre…"

"I'm going to make you comfortable enough to be your-self around me."

Closing the space between us for the last time, I lifted her off of her feet and laid her gently in the middle of my California king.

Her hands found my shoulders while I went back to kissing her slowly. Those full lips, her neck, collarbone, breast, navel, and her honeycomb. My hands pushed her legs as far back as they would go. I devoured her, caressed her bud, pulled orgasms from her core that she didn't know existed.

Kendra hadn't been loved properly. No one was taking care of her, but tonight I was going to change that. I had something for her that was going to shed those layers of uncertainty away.

Her toes curled and pointed to the ceiling. A series of oohs, aah's, and whimpers escaped from her mouth into the space around us.

She was trying to catch her breath when I came back up to kiss her lips. "Turn over."

She didn't ask or hesitate; she grabbed a pillow, flipped over and stuck it under her belly. I massaged her back before I laid my body to side, so she wouldn't have to support all of my weight. Slowly, inching inside of her, I watched as she gripped the sheets.

"Oh my – ahh," she moaned into the mattress. "What are you doing to me?"

I hadn't even got started.

Grinding in and out of her, the only noises to be heard in this room and probably down the hall, were the sounds of her gushing all over me and these sheets and those sexy slurs from her lips.

From her stomach to her back, Kendra held me securely to her body. My forehead was pressed against hers and my lips had taken custody of her again.

I was so focused on making her understand this dick wasn't for everyone and if she wanted all of it, she could have it. Lil' mama had me in here thinking I was Keith Sweat.

"Who's gon to love you like me?" I quizzed, feeling her walls quiver. She was almost there.

"Nobody," she whimpered.

"Who's gon touch you like me?"

"Nobody. Baby."

"Who's gon fuck you like Dre?"

"No. Body," she growled, clawing at my body. "You're going fuck my head up."

I kissed her as she came. "Nah, I'm going take all the shit away. I got you."

I didn't even think twice about pulling out. It was going to be what it was going to be. Kendra could either come into this willingly, or through a kid. Either way, I was cool with it.

I watched her sleep, sprawled out in my sheets. This was a sight I was going to get used to.

9

KENDRA

I felt like I ran in a marathon. My everything hurt. I wasn't sure if there was a part of my body that hadn't fell victim to DeAndre's amazing sex. I wasn't quite ready to call it love making, but I knew that's what it was. There was a different connection last night. There was some form of magic that danced in dimness of the room.

My skin tingled in reaction to his lips and his fingers touching every inch of me. The hot water hitting my skin, caused me to moan lowly. We woke up, realizing we fell asleep in the center of our mess. While Dre changed the sheets and prepared himself for tomorrow's game, I stood in his shower letting the water run over me.

In two days, I was going to be home and dealing with my real life again. I didn't want to go back. For the moments I was wrapped up in Dre, I believed that this was where I was supposed to be. As unconventional as this whole thing had been, it felt amazing.

It felt refreshing.

I didn't care about who he was or what he had. He saw past everything, made me hesitant, and just made me forget. I forgot about the pain I felt before I got here, and I sure as hell didn't want to go back and deal with any of the craziness.

I was so deep in my thoughts; I didn't hear the door to shower open or Dre step in. But when he wrapped his arms around my naked body and kissed my bare shoulder, I came back into focus.

The sweet moment was short lived as he jumped back from me. "Gahdamn! What the hell are you doing in here? Boiling neck bones or some shit? Why the hell is the water so hot?"

"It's not even that hot," I said with a giggle at his reaction.

"Shit," he scoffed and walked over to the other end of the shower and turned the water on.

"Keep your hell water over there, Satan," he taunted over his shoulder.

"You know good and well -"

Turning around to face me, he smirked. "What? That you ain't? You got to be practicing some dark shit to have me out here like this."

I rolled my eyes.

"Say you ain't. Your sex is better than sin, you make me fall in worship, you got me taking showers with you. That's a power that I know better than to disturb. Kendra ...you are a unformidable type of love."

I looked at him as he rubbed the soap over his body. I wanted to lick him. I wanted to do and be whatever he wanted. My stomach flipped, turned and knotted, unleashing a wave of nerves I couldn't contain or control. It was strong; I thought I was going to pass out.

"And you aren't? You have undone my entire being. I don't submit to anything. The idea of it wards me off. But you, Dre...you make me want to give you all of me willingly. Five days...how the hell did you do that in five days?"

He smiled so wide that I could see his pearly white teeth. "How many times am I gon have to tell you this? Huh? Stop looking at my dick and listen to me. Hear me good. I be knowing."

The second I rolled my eyes, smiled at him, and took a step closer, the bathroom door flew open. "I knew it! I knew it! I knew it! I KNEW IT! How dare y'all!"

Micah screeched so loud, it made me jump and damn near slip and fall face flat on the tile. If it weren't for me grabbing the rail of the shower, I would have bust my ass.

"What is your nosey ass doing in here!" DeAndre shouted. "Get out."

"No!" Micah screeched back, in the most dramatic tone of voice she possessed. I wasn't going to hear the end of this. She was going to hold this over my head until the day she died, probably.

I could see her through the fogged glass. I knew she was standing in the middle of the bathroom with her face twisted and her neck rolling. Her hands were probably on her hips like she was my mother.

"Mimi, get out," I huffed.

"Don't you dare Mimi, me! You been fucking my brother! I brought you here to let your hair down not get it pulled, or whatever freaky shit y'all been doing behind my back!"

"Why is she so damn loud?" he groaned, turning the water off.

I shrugged my shoulders and did the same. Grabbing a towel, I wrapped it securely around my body. "She's your sister. All y'all are loud."

"Don't get me started on you," he threw over his shoulder while wrapping the towel over his waist and stepping out.

"That's how we ended up in the situation," I mumbled, following him out the shower. "I can't believe you are standing in here."

Micah scoffed, gripped her imaginary pearls, and looked at DeAndre and I like we went off and got married without her knowing.

"You know what I can't believe?" she started, turning her dramatics up a notch. "That you really out bussin' it open for him."

"What you rather her bust it open for one of them lame niggas y'all got in VA?" Dre commented, causing both of us to flash him a look. "I'm gon let you two handle this."

"Yeah, you do that. And don't go far, I'll be out to cuss you out too," Micah replied as Dre walked out, chuckling to himself. "So, when did this start? Hmm?"

I rolled my eyes again and moved my wet hair out of my face. "How important is that?"

"Very damn important. At the least, I was expecting an "Oh girl your brother is fine." So, I could have told you, that my brother is a gentle giant with a big ass mouth, who needs someone like you in his life because up until now, every woman he's crossed has had foul ass intentions. But you didn't give me that opportunity, did you?"

I chuckled lightly and shook my head. This girl was a damn trip. "Well, Mi—"

"Aht!" She threw up her hand. "I am not talking to you for another two hours because I'm upset that I wasn't the love connection in all of this. And I've lapped this big ass house four times looking for you. Get dressed, we need help cooking dinner for tomorrow."

Micah turned on her heels and stomped out the room with her nose tooted up in the air.

"That girl is ridiculous," I muttered to myself before grabbing another towel to dry my hair.

Dre walked back in the bathroom in black Nike sweatpants and his team dri fit shirt. "You good?"

"Yeah, I'm used to her dramatics. I'm going to go downstairs and help with dinner for tomorrow."

"Her loud ass ruined what I wanted to do to you." He smirked softly and hooked my chin with those magic wands he called fingers. With a soft kiss to my lips, he lightly bit my bottom lip.

"You should preserve your energy; you have a big game tomorrow. I don't want to get yelled at again because you were sluggish."

"True, they ain't gon' let you live that one down at all." He chuckled and kissed my lips one last time before stepping away. "Make sure my food is good, too. You better put your toes in my shit and wiggle them thangs."

I laughed with a snort. "Why are you this way?"

"You like that shit, stop frontin'. Go put some clothes on you before I bend your ass over and eat breakfast."

I had never been to any sort of sports event professionally. This was so much different from any college game I'd been to. The energy in the stadium was live and contagious. I stood beside Mr. Yates, who promised to notify me when to cheer and when to cuss out the refs.

DeAndre had been sure to make sure we had the best seats in the house--for them. I would have preferred to be in the sky box where the food was but nevertheless, here we were. We all wore custom jerseys with gloves and beanie hats to match. Being with the four for them was probably the most fun I had in a very long time. Despite my own parents not reaching out to me once since leaving the states, the Yates made me feel like I was family. I couldn't have asked for anything more.

The game progressed with DeAndre's team down by three points and the anxiousness in the stadium raised. Even I felt it. I knew how much it would mean to him and his family to go home with the win tonight. There were only two minutes left on the clock and Mr. Yate gripped my hand as tight as he could.

"Anything can happen in two minutes," he spoke over the noise of the stadium. "This is when you pray that coach has some damn sense and let's ya man there run it in."

My man.

"Instead of passing it, right?"

"Right, they're too damn close to pass it. It would be stupid to do that. Dre can literally skip into the endzone if the play is called right."

Micah and Mrs. Yates were both standing up with their knuckles pressed to their lips. The clock counted down the seconds. The quarterback looked from side to side, trying to find his receiver to throw it to before time ran out. Something happened; a receiver cut through the defensive line, drawing everyone's attention to him as the quarterback slipped Dre the ball letting him run it straight into the endzone.

The crowd went completely bananas. Mr. Yates let go of my hand and kissed my cheek. While the rest of them embrace one another, I watched Dre toss the ball to the crowd, and pointed to the sky before being tackled by his team.

Micah jumped on me and cheered. "You just might be his good luck charm."

I smiled and hugged her back, but I wasn't taking credit for it. That was all Dre.

10

DEANDRE

I was tired, excited, and irritated all at once.

I played my ass off today. I had to put a good show on because she was watching me from the stands. The second I walked out for warm-ups and spotted Kendra front and center wearing my jersey with an infectious smile on her face, I knew I had to make this the best game she'd ever seen. It helped distract me from the fact she would be gone in less than twenty-four hours. I was in my feelings heavy.

"Kendra, ain't no way you can tell me that people aren't booking you up back in Virginia." Pops sat back and rubbed his belly. "Mama was the last woman to cook like that and put me to sleep."

"It was great not to have to cook all this with you standing over me," Ma commented, standing up from the table, grabbing our plates. She looked at Kendra and smiled warmly. "Don't make this the last time we spend time with you. Dre see to it."

I smirked and looked at Kendra blush before Micah smacked her lips. "Y'all know she's my friend, right?"

"And you can have her back tomorrow," I replied, making Micah rolled her eyes.

"I guess it's safe to say that you ain't coming shopping with us," Micah shot Kendra look. As jealous as she was with me taking up Kendra's time, she couldn't hide the smile that was trying to cross her face.

"You don't look that upset to me," Kendra commented, catching it too. "Your sneaky ass was probably planning this anyway."

"Well after that busta you left at home, you needed to be in the presence of a real one. So, for the sake of you enjoying yourself, I'll let you live and have tonight." Micah scoffed like the brat she was.

"I don't know what you thought was gon' happen, baby girl. I saw how they looked at each when she got here. Some things just work out like that," Pops said before standing up from the table.

Micah huffed again. "Dre, you should be thanking me."

"I did all the hard work," I defended, furrowing my brow.

Micah's face frowned. "I don't want to know that."

"On that note," Mom spoke up. "We're going to clean up. Can you two help before disappearing?"

"Yeah, be useful for once this week."

"Boy," I started. "You get on my damn nerves, you know."

Micah shot a sinister look at me like she was up to no good. "Don't act like I didn't see Jermel up in your face after the game. Don't fuck around and get his ass beat."

Her look intensified. "How about I let you and Kendra mind your business, and I mind mine."

If I wasn't trying to get this table and kitchen clean so I could enjoy the rest of my night, I would have snatched Micah's tracks out her head. She knew how to get people beat up for her. Teammate or not, I wasn't playing about her.

"Now, Kendra can I have some of your attention before you end up tied up."

That wasn't a bad idea at all.

Once everything was clean, Ma and Micah headed out to go spend Pops' hard-earned money and a lot of mine.

Pops was in the living room with his shirt pulled over his stomach, and piece of pie resting on it.

"He done ate himself into a coma," I laughed and grabbed a jacket and blanket out the hall closet.

"Are you going to leave him like that?" Kendra asked, pulling her boots over her cute ass feet.

I looked back at him and nodded. "Hell yeah. I tried to move his food one year and got hit in the face. I ain't fuckin' with it. You ready?"

She nodded her head. "Where are we going?"

"Walking off that good ass food you made."

She followed me blindly, which meant I had her trust. Her body was mine--I made sure of that--now all I needed was her heart.

Trailing her out of the house, I draped the blanket over her coat. She got cold easily; I picked up on that and being I slept the night before with a corner of the blanket, I made a mental note of it. We walked silently for a minute down the lit path that lead to the most peaceful part of my estate.

"So, I think you've turned me into a fan." She broke the silence and leaned into me more.

"That's what I was trying to do. Had me out there showing out."

She chuckled softly. "You and your tricks."

"I got a lot more, baby."

Kendra sighed heavily and dropped her head.

"What?"

"...Tomorrow I go back to reality." Her voice got low and somber. Her voice mirrored how I felt inside.

I stopped walking and pulled her into me. "I could say some fly shit and make you stay here, but I know you got a life out there. But I want you in mine, too. This doesn't have to end here, you know that, right?"

"I know it, but I don't want to –"

"You don't want to what? If you are talking about falling for me, you did that. You're just trying to fight that. Stop it. It doesn't have to make sense. There's a lot of things in my life that didn't make sense, but it's just what God intended for it to me. I don't question him. I was a seventh round draft pick, I spent my first season on the bench. One game changed my life, now I'm starting and got more money that I know what to do with. I was supposed to be another statistic in jail cell somewhere."

"Wow," she spoke up, looking into my eyes with admiration.

"Yeah, so I know that this," I started up again, pointing at the both of us. "Ain't a fly by night kinda thing. I'm gon' miss you, but you'll be back."

"You're so sure."

I snickered, kissed her lips and said, "Hell yeah. In a week, in Arizona. Don't even fight it, I've already got your ticket."

"You know what?" she spoke slowly as she pulled away from me. I was hoping that she wasn't going to find another reason in her head why this wouldn't work.

"I know that if you're about to say something that is remotely close to 'this ain't gon work' I don't want to hear it. I know that if you're going to tell me that you still got something going on at home with that –"

Kendra started walking away from me, which only set me off more. "You really think you know, huh?"

"Because I do."

"No, Dre," she threw over her shoulder. "You don't."

"Then what were you going to say?" I released with a grunt, not wanting to go back and forth with her. Not tonight. If she weren't leaving in the morning, I wouldn't mind going back and forth and shutting her up.

Kendra wrapped the blanket around herself tighter before turning around to look me up and down. She bit her lip at the corner, looked me up and down like she was undressing me with those golden eyes that danced underneath the moonlight. "I was going to say that this blanket just isn't doing the trick anymore. So, do you want to spend the night worried about how tomorrow is goodbye for now, or how tonight is hello for as long as you can have me? It's really all up to you."

Dragging the tip of my tongue over my bottom lip, I watched as she walked back to the house.

"Mm," I grunted, grabbing my dick that she raised with her last set of words.

When I got to the house, Pops was still passed out with the same piece of pie resting on his gut. I shook my head with a chuckle and climbed the stairs to my room. Pushing the door open, I wasn't expecting to see Kendra laying in the middle of my bed waiting on me. I felt like a kid on Christmas morning.

"Damn," I hissed, locking the door.

I moved to the end of the bed and studied her in the black lace bra and panty set. "You're not in control tonight."

"Nah."

She chuckled and sat up on her knees. Kendra got closer to me and ran her hand along my jawline, giving me a light smack. My face twisted. If she did that shit again, I was going to tie her ass up and show her what submission was.

"I said, you're not in control tonight. Understand?"

Fuck it. I was going to see where this went. "Aight."

"Good." She climbed off that bed and walked around me like I was her prey. "Get naked."

Quickly, I started pulling my shirt off.

"Uh uh, slowly, baby."

I laughed lightly and followed her rules. Slowly peeling my shirt over my head, I stepped out my sweats, and then pulled my boxers off.

She licked her lips hungrily. "Good, boy."

"Boy?"

"I didn't tell you that you could talk, did I?"

I tightened my jaw and lowly watched as she pranced around the room, picking up my clothes off the floor and putting them in their respective places. Kendra then pulled her curly hair into a high bun.

"Get in the bed, lay on your back, and don't move."

I did as she said. I noticed that she had a few of my ties laid out on the nightstand. Kendra climbed her thick ass on top of me and took my hands and placed them over my head. "The rule of this game is no touching. You can't touch me, but I can touch you wherever I want to."

"Kendra."

"DeAndre, shut up."

She tied my hands together tighter than any pair of handcuffs I ever wore. "I'll untie you when I think you're ready."

She kissed me slowly. I was already harder than a brick. If she kept teasing me like this, I was going to bust without her even doing anything. Kendra kissed my lips, then my neck. I was too big to be in this bed moaning like a bitch. Every so often she would bite down on my flesh then caress the spot with her lips or tongue. She did this as she went over my abs till she got to my dick.

Running her tongue along my length, she chuckled, watching my body tense up. I was expecting her to swallow me whole. She didn't. She kissed and bit down on my thighs, making me wince. I'd never been on the receiving end of pleasure and pain before. Just when I was about to buck her ass off of me, she took me into her mouth and started giving me head like it was her job.

"Shhhhiitttttt," I hissed, wanting to put my hands in her hair.

Popping my dick out her mouth, she spit on it, looked me in my eyes and started again. I was touching the back of throat; she gagged, but that didn't stop her. Kendra was sucking my dick with no hands. She had my shit soaked.

"Mm," she moaned, slurping up the excess saliva and going back at it.

"I'm gon nut."

"Do it," she slurred.

I would have never expected this woman, who looked like a good girl, to be such a freak. If she was bringing it like this now, what was she going to later on?

She kept her same rhythm with her hands pressed against my thighs. My whole body tensed up before I shot my nut down her throat.

"Mmhmm," she hummed. Kendra sucked me until I was dry.

"Gahdamn, lil mama. Let me out this shit."

She chuckled. "No."

She out the bed and disappeared into the bathroom. I needed this moment to breath and get myself ready for whatever she was bringing next.

er
AUBREE PYNN

When she walked out of the bathroom, she had a bottle of oil in her hands. Starting with my feet, she massaged my body all the way up to my neck.

"Let me taste that pussy."

"Do you have manners?"

"Yea."

"Use them."

"Let taste that pussy, please."

Hovering herself over my face, I moved her panties to the side with my teeth before burying my face into that sweet honeycomb. Rolling her hips over my face, she let me drag my tongue from the front to the back; the back to the front. I sucked her pearl until it was swollen, and she let that honey drip all over my face.

"I'm ready, get this shit off of me."

Her eyes were low. She was still riding through the cosmos as she untied me and dropped the ties on me.

Relinquishing control, she waited for my command. "Flip that ass over, toot it up, and put your hands behind your back."

"My pleasure," she replied like she worked at Chick-Fil-A.

84

After her hands were secured behind her back, I pulled her bun loose, and held on to her hips while I slid inside of her. I grunted, she moaned. Filling her up, I pumped in and out slowly making her cum within minutes.

"Give it all to me, Dre," she slurred.

"All of it?"

"Every inch, baby."

"Say less." I grabbed ahold of the knot I made with the tie and picked up my pace. I slammed this dick into her the way she asked for it.

She cursed into the pillow, occasionally she bit it trying to keep her loud ass moaning muffled. Throwing that ass back at me, she looked over her shoulder.

"Whose pussy is it?"

"Yours! It's all yours!"

"You're fucking right is. You want to cum?"

She lost her breath for a moment. "Y-yes. Please."

"Then cum for Daddy. I want to see that pussy cream on this dick."

After a few more strokes; she shook, gasped for air as I wrapped my hand lightly around her throat and coated my dick with her love. "There you go baby. Mm, that pussy so pretty when it cums for daddy."

Kendra fell straight on her stomach after I pulled out and untied her.

I climbed off the bed and went into the bathroom. I ran a bath; we both needed to relax after that. Returning to the room to scoop her up in my arms, I carried her into the bathroom.

"You should be sleeping," she spoke up after we got settled into the hot water.

"I can't sleep knowing you're leaving soon. I'll sleep when after you get on a plane."

She ran her hand softly over mine while her head rested on my chest. "Thank you."

Kissing the top of her curls, I replied, "Nah, thank you."

11

KENDRA

"Wake up, baby," Dre's soft baritone met my ears. I didn't want to wake up. I didn't want to remove my body out his bed. I knew I had to. I had to get up and get back to my life.

I slowly opened my eyes and looked at him. He was so beautiful, especially being the first thing that I saw in the morning.

DeAndre looked at me like I was the most beautiful woman in the world. Reaching up to touch his face, I smiled. "I'm going to miss you."

"We'll be together soon." He wrapped his hand around mine and kissed the back of my hand. "Your flight leaves in two hours, go pack."

I sat up and huffed. "If I can walk."

"You probably can't. I did that on purpose."

"Of course, you did."

I scooted out the bed and walked out of the room. I had to drag myself down to my room that I rarely slept in.

My phone was buzzing across the nightstand. I should have turned it off, so I didn't have to deal with it. Gary had been blowing me up since yesterday. Why I hadn't blocked all his numbers, was beyond me. It was a lapse of my judgement. Before I got on the plane and flew out the Dallas, my heart wasn't completely closed to him. Now, I wanted nothing to do with him.

"What do you want?" I finally answered the phone.

"Where the fuck are you? You lost your fucking mind disappearing on me. Who is this nigga you with?" he sounded off. He was so loud that if I dropped the phone on the bed and walked out the room, I could still hear him loud and clear.

"I'm not doing this. I didn't answer, so you could scream and berate me."

"Answer the fucking question, Kendra. Who is this nigga you with?"

Micah must have taken pictures of me with everyone and tagged me on social media. That's the only way he would have known that I was with someone else, let alone enjoying myself enough to drive him to new realms of crazy.

He'd yelled before, pushed me into walls, but he had never reached this point. "Does he know that you loved me and that you will always love me. If you say you didn't, you're a liar."

I needed to hang up before I succumbed to his bullying again. I'd gotten away from it. I finally got away from it, but I was feeling small again. My voice was fleeting. I couldn't let him steal it again.

"No, it's no lie that I loved you. But I don't love you anymore. I'm sorry I ever did." I was getting choked up and a knock came across the door. "I have to go."

Hanging up, I quickly wiped my face and powered my phone off.

"Come in."

"You ready, girl?" Micah asked.

I shook my head, sure to hide my face from her. "Yeah, I just have some stuff to grab out the bathroom."

"You were in here with Dre?"

"No," I answered.

"Hm, he just walked away from your door. I thought y'all was in here being nasty. I shrugged it off and went to get the rest of my stuff. Thirty minutes later, I was packed and ready to go.

Dre hadn't said much to me since he carried my stuff to his pick-up. His face was tight, and he was withdrawn.

"Micah let me know when y'all get home," Mrs. Yates spoke up as she hugged me. "Kendra, don't be a stranger. You're family now."

I smiled. "Thank you for making me feel like I was at home."

"You did that. You fit right in."

She released me and stood on the porch by Mr. Yates, who watched us, initially to make sure we got in the car without an issue.

I climbed into the passenger seat after Micah took the back seat and stretched out. Dre climbed in and pulled off. He said nothing, he didn't even look at me. Maybe this was his way of processing it, but I didn't like it. Not after I knew how warm and open, he could be.

I clasped my hands together in my lab and stared out the window until we pulled up to the airport. My heart started to beat with anxiety. I knew I was going to see him in a week, but that didn't change how I was feeling.

I slid out his jacked up pick-up truck and waited for him to hand me my bags. I learned not to touch anything remotely heavy. A luxury I wish I could take with me. Dre handed Micah her bags, hugged her tightly before her kissing her cheek and telling her to behave herself. Then he flashed his eyes at me. He looked at me like I stole his damn dog.

"Here, this was cool. I guess I should let you go back to that dude you love."

I dropped my head. "You heard the phone call."

"Yeah, I wish I didn't."

"Dre, it wasn't like that I swear," I started, looking back up at him. "I only answered the phone to tell him that –"

"That what?" He peered down at me with a stern expression. "To tell him what, Kendra?"

"That I was done. Dre, I don't—"

"You can save it. I knew this shit was too good to be true. Who the hell was I fooling thinking that I could make you do anything, when you still have him hanging in the wind? It's always you pretty ones. You innocent looking women, who cause the most damage."

"Dre let up, it's not like that," Micah spoke up for me because my mouth had stopped working.

My eyes were welling with tears. "I promise you, it wasn't like that."

"You think I'm going to be stupid enough to hang around and find out. Nah," he said before dropping my bags at my feet.

"Dre, please don't do this," I pleaded, taking a few steps behind him, but Micah grabbed my arm.

"Stop it. You are not going to chase a man, whether it's my brother or not. Let him cool off, he'll cool off. Pull yourself together."

I heard her, but I couldn't. Dre climbed back in his truck and pulled away from the curb. I felt like I was coming apart at the seams. It felt like he took my heart out my chest as he pulled off. "I just wanted him to hear me. I would never tell Gary I loved him after everything he did to me."

I was breaking down, I felt it. I didn't want to be out here in the cold crying and snotting behind a man that could walk away from me so easily after picking me apart.

Using the back of my hand to wipe my face, I took a deep breath before picking up my bags and walking into the airport with Micah.

"It's going to be fine. He'll come around; I promise he will."

Promises meant nothing to me at this point. I just had to take the cards as life dealt them to me. I should have trusted my first mind and kept my ass away from DeAndre, literally. My heart couldn't go through the ringer again.

The entire trip back home seemed like an eternity. When we got back to the house, I went straight to my room for the next week and laid in the middle of the bed. Laying here without Dre's arms draped over me seemed so foreign and unnatural.

I powered my phone back on, curious to see if he reached out to apologize. Nothing at all.

I got on social media to see if he might've posted some passive aggressive shit. He blocked me.

With a heavy sigh, I scrolled through my phone and blocked all of Gary's numbers. Then I chose to text my parents, who hadn't sent anything at all.

I hope your Thanksgiving was nice. I wish y'all were here...I'm okay. I guess we'll talk when y'all decide to come home.

Tossing my phone across the room, I let my tears fall and soak the pillow. I needed to let it all out. Gary's bullshit, Dre's attitude, my disappointment with myself and the loneliness I felt.

My sobs must've alarmed Micah. She walked in and crawled in bed with me. "Come here."

I rolled over and laid on her lap.

"Everything is going to work out. Life, love, and business will be okay."

I must've cried myself to sleep. When I woke up, Micah was sleep on one side of the bed and I was balled up on the other side. Rolling over to my back, I looked up at the ceiling. Before I could get myself back to sleep, my notifications started going off again.

With a heavy groan, I grabbed my phone to see deposits, email inquiries, and referrals. Micah must have had a direct line to God because He definitely moved faster than I thought He would. He came through in the clutch for me. I was definitely going to have to be a bedside Baptist in the morning and give Him some thanks.

My pity party ended as I reached under the bed to pull my laptop out. Dre would just have to be a memory for when I had time to think about him. I was going to be incredibly busy. I needed that distraction and the money.

12

DEANDRE

I dragged myself out of the locker room with my head hung low. I felt like shit. I fumbled the ball and that cost us the wild card game. On top of all that, I was missing the hell out of Kendra. I didn't mean to go off on her the way I did. My feelings were everywhere. I didn't even bother hearing her side. When her eyes started to fill with tears, I had to walk away. I didn't want to, but I had to. I couldn't handle seeing her tears.

I had it so bad, I got home and blocked her on everything. I couldn't be tempted to reach out after I showed my ass at the airport.

My guilt prompted me to tweet out her business, in hopes that the pain I caused emotionally, could be made up with money. I knew better. No amount of money could fix what I did. I didn't give a shit about losing the game. She wasn't here to squeal, hug me, and tell me how exciting it was. That shit gave me life. She gave me life. Those seven days were the most alive I'd felt in a long time.

I wanted her back in my arms, but I wasn't sure how bad me ghosting her messed with her.

When I got to my car, Micah was blowing up my line. I really didn't want to talk to her about this game, but I wanted to know how Kendra was doing, so I answered.

"Don't say it," I started roughly.

"I wasn't going to tell you what you already know. Your head wasn't in that game at all," she replied with a scoff. "Where was your head, Dre?"

"Is that all you called me for?"

"Yeah. You played like shit and the temper tantrum you threw in the third quarter was a mess. You know it."

I rolled my eyes. "Gee, thanks."

"You're a grown ass man, Dre. You know Mom is going to call and fuss at you about this."

"Please don't remind me," I replied, pinching the bridge of my nose.

"Too late," she sassed. "You miss her, don't you?"

"Miss who?" I asked, playing stupid.

Hell yeah, I missed her.

"Keep playing with me like you are as dumb as they want you to be," she fired back. "You need to get your ass on a plane and get out here. You need to make this right."

"Is she okay?" I questioned with pure concern.

Micah sighed. "I saw your tweet. I didn't tell her you're the reason she's so busy, but she's not slowing down. I don't think she's slept. All she does is work. She ain't eating, Dre."

"Damn," I blew.

"Yeah. When Kendra gets like this, she buries it under a bunch of other shit. You were dead ass wrong with how you handled that shit," Micah continued to put me in my place.

I sighed. "I know."

"Then why ain't you make it right? It's been two weeks."

"I wanted to give her some space."

Micah smacked her lips. "Bullshit, boy. Your ass was embarrassed for assuming and you made an ass out of her and you. She don't want that fuck boy back. You would have known that if you heard her out. He was a piece of work."

"He was that bad?"

"It's not my business to tell, Dre. If you want to know, you'll be out here. You don't have nothing else to do."

I groaned, toying with the thought of flying out to Virginia and begging Kendra to forgive me after showing my ass the way I did. If I went out there, I had to be on my game one hundred percent. She didn't need sex to convenience her. She needed me to own up to my shit and show her that I really wanted this. That I really wanted us.

"She still staying with you?" I asked, trying to get a game plan.

"Nope, she moved out two days ago. She has events lined up all weekend."

Resting my head against the steering wheel, I let out a huff and rubbed my temples.

Micah started up again. "Alright, you're slow, so I'm going to help you out here. You fly out here get a room, and I'll set it up from there. Okay?"

"What did I do to deserve you?" I smirked after asking that question.

"Shut up boy, this ain't for you. This is for my best friend. I saw her smile for the first time in years. I saw how alive she came when she was with you. As much as I hate how you stole her from me. You make her happy, so it's only right I make sure she's with who makes her heart happy."

Micah could be a pain in my ass most of the time, but she had a heart of gold. I was almost inclined to fall back and let her do her thing with Jermel. That was still up in the air though. I had to see how this shit was going to turn out with Kendra.

After a few minutes of thinking this over, I agreed. "I'll take the jet out there."

"Alright, where would you like me to book you room?"

"It's Norfolk, don't put me in the ghetto, please."

"Listen, money has changed you."

I laughed and started my engine. "Girl, shut up. You know damn well I ain't putting myself in a position to go to jail over shit."

"Don't I know it," she said in a sarcastic tone. "Book your own room. She has to come to my house to get the rest of her stuff anyway. Either way, I'll make sure you get to say your peace."

"You aight sometimes."

"I'm alright all the time. What the hell you thought this was?"

"Aight, Micah, bye."

I hung up and headed to my apartment to pack my duffle and calling my pilot. Here went nothing. I was nervous as hell like I hadn't been in and out of her for almost a week. This was different. No more impulsive emotions, I needed to let her know what was up. Kendra had me wrapped around her finger and my heart in the palm of her hands. I didn't want it back though; I just want her in my arms.

13

KENDRA

"Hey, we need some more mac and cheese on the buffet," I directed a few members of my staff. "Could one of you make sure all the drinks are refilled? Remember, the happier they are, the more they'll come back."

Two members of my team broke off and went to take care of the things I asked for. I knew they were tired; we'd been going nonstop for two weeks straight. The bookings were still rolling in. As of now, I was booked all the way through April. Which was great; I finally had some stability to stand on my own without needing anyone. I went from my parents' care into Gary's after trying to find myself.

I was thankful that that part of my life was over, but I wasn't really looking forward for the next chapter. Especially, if it didn't include DeAndre. I'd been putting the thought of him out of my head. Working made that a little easier to do. I don't know what he did to me. I couldn't figure out if it was his charm, slick ass mouth, or the magic his did to my body. Either way, I was a goner.

It was almost pathetic how I looked for him in every man that smiled in my face. I didn't find anything remotely close. No one possessed half the qualities he did. After seven days, I knew what kind of man I found myself wrapped up with. A man unlike any I had before. He had me in my bag.

Shit, he still did.

I was emotional standing in the back of the room by the kitchen, looking over my third banquet with tears threatening to spill over the brim of my eyes. I sucked in a deep breath, shut my eyes and shook the wave of emotion off.

I was a professional and DeAndre Yates wasn't going to have me out here crying in public over him. My willpower wouldn't let me.

Peeling myself away from the spot I was planted in, I started walking around the perimeter of the room to make sure everything was flowing smoothly. The team was buzzing around the buffet to keep it fully stocked and refreshed. My shoulders relaxed a bit.

"Ma'am, could I get some more bread at table seven?" The voice that rang out against my ears made every hair on my body stand on its ends. The wave of nervousness was quickly replaced with irritation after I laid my eyes on him.

"Why are you here?" I skipped over the part where I faked like I wasn't hurt by his actions. "I'm working."

"Give me ten minutes," he said, but his eyes pleaded with me.

For the sake of remaining as professional as I could, I smiled and talked through my teeth. "DeAndre, I'm working. I don't have ten minutes to give you."

I found it funny that he wanted ten minutes and couldn't give me two. I missed him, yes, but was I going to let him make a mess of me again, no.

"If not now then when?" he asked, closing the gap between us.

I took a step back and shrugged my shoulders. "I don't know. Let me get to you in two weeks. I got shit I have to do."

Dre apparently didn't care that I was working, he stepped and scoffed. "That's petty."

I shrugged again and turned to walk away. I wasn't doing this with him.

My attention went back to finishing the event. Once it was over, my team had everything broken down, cleaned, and packed in the back of my SUV. All the extra tips we got tonight, I divvied it out and sent them home with a little extra.

When I got home, I spotted Micah's car parked on the curb. That only meant that she was inside, more than likely with her brother. I really wasn't in the mood; all I wanted to do was sleep. I knew that wasn't going to happen. Dre wanted to get back in my good graces and Micah's nosey ass was going to stay around until it happened.

The walk to my front door of the townhome I rented was more like a slow drag. I put my key in the lock and rolled my eyes. I could hear Micah's loud ass through the door.

Pushing the door open, I spotted them on the couch and said, "When I gave you that key, it was for emergencies. Not this."

Micah kissed her teeth and brought the wine glass to her lips. "This is an emergency."

"I know good and damn well that ain't my wine that was unopened this morning," I groaned, completely ignoring Dre sitting on my couch.

I stepped right over him and went to the kitchen to take a look at the spread that Micah made for herself. "You got to be kidding me."

"No, actually I'm not. You two are stubborn, and I could be here all night. I needed some snacks to get through this."

"Ain't nothing to get through," I said, peeling my jacket off my arms. "I'm good."

I could feel his eyes glaring at me from where he sat. I refused to look at him. I would be putty within minutes. Dre needed to know that what he did wasn't okay with me, and I wasn't going to just let him off the hook.

"You lie like a rug and you know it," Micah said with a huff. "Dre, tell her what you need to tell her."

"He doesn't need to say anything to me. I said, I was good."

I kicked off my shoes and climbed the stairs to my bedroom. I knew he was going to burst through the door in five seconds. He couldn't control himself.

"Five, four, three, two, one."

The door flew open.

"I'm not about to be going back and forth with you all night," he sounded off.

"Then don't. You didn't want to hear me, then; I don't need to hear you now. I really meant what I said, I'm good. It was good while it lasted, right?"

He clenched his jaw. "Kendra."

"What?" I turned around to look at him. His eyes were sad. "Don't play on my emotions, man."

He sighed and stepped further into the room before shutting the door. "I'm not. I was wrong. Dead ass wrong for how I acted."

"Tuh," I blew with a scoff. "You think? I've been treated like shit for years, Dre. I've been slammed into walls, barked at like a dog, belittled and I got out that shit. I'm not going back to that shit. I'm not going to let you treat me like that, no matter how hurt you are."

"Baby, I —"

I threw my hand up. "I'm not done."

He huffed and fell back. "Had you heard me out, you would have known that little dumbass had been calling like a mad man and was screaming about some pictures he saw of us. He said that I loved him, and I was coming back."

"Well?"

I squinted my eyes and chuckled. "Do you see him? If that was the case, I would have never ended up in your bed."

"I fucked up."

"You did," I replied with a shrug of my shoulders.

Dre invaded my space, taking my breath away. I wanted to stay mad at him. I wanted to hold on to this anger as long as I could. At least that way, I wouldn't get stupid over him.

"You got my mind fucked up, Kendra."

His tone was smoother than silk and his touch was softer than cashmere, but he still managed to send currents through my body. Dre's large hand rested on the side of my face while he looked at me intently. "I knew you were going to have me out here like a mad man. Jealous of the jeans you wear because the only thing I want hugging that sweet ass is me. I knew I would hate the idea of all of your former lovers having you, 'cause you're mine. Lil' mama got me trippin' over everything just to get back to you. I am so sorry. I fumbled and that's on me. I ain't trying to do this shit without you."

"Be gentle with me, Dre," I spoke against his lips. "I only require to be a beast when it comes to my protection and my kitty."

"Speaking of which," he started.

I chuckled, kissed his lips, grabbed him through his sweats. "No, you're in time out."

"Does this time out involve you smothering me with that pussy?" he slurred before kissing my lips again.

"Ewww, y'all nasty!" Micah snickered from the other side of the door.

"Gahdamn, Micah!" he growled.

I laughed and pulled myself away from him. "She's not going to leave. Let's go give her needy ass some attention and hope that leaves by the morning."

"Yeah, right. Watch she's going to crawl her ass right in the middle of us tonight," he groaned, on the verge of having a fit.

"Who said you were sleeping in here?"

DeAndre scoffed, wrapped my wrist in his hand before grabbing a handful of my ass. "I heard that shit purring, don't play."

"That's enough!" Micah started again. "We got snacks to eat and movies to watch."

FOUR MONTHS LATER

14

DeAndre

"Boy, look at my boy in there," I cheered, walking around the property with Kendra.

Spring had come and everything around the estate was bright green. No matter how much pollen was out here, she came out to walk every day.

"We don't know if it's a boy or a girl, yet," she reminded me. "Don't get your hopes up and be disappointed when there's pink everywhere."

"I will have to get more guns. I ain't playing that shit," I rebutted with a scoff.

I didn't know what the hell Kendra found to be so funny. She knew as crazy as I was about her, I would be even crazier if our baking bun was a girl. I couldn't even handle the idea of no nappy headed little boys chasing after her. Everyone associated with him would have to take this bullet.

"When is this expensive ass gender reveal taking place anyway?" I told Micah and Ma that money wasn't an issue when it came down to what Kendra wanted for this gender reveal. They apparently took that to the head and lost their damn minds.

"Don't you even take that tone with me, Dre. I told you I was fine with a cake, but Yates one and Yates two insisted we have a party. They got my parents flying in and all. I was really okay with a quiet evening," she corrected me with a point of the finger before rubbing her growing belly.

She glowed. I wasn't sure she could shine any brighter. I loved having her with me every day.

A lot had happened in four months. I got traded to Dallas, which was cool with me. On top of her finding that I purposely trapped her ass, her business was booming to the point where she could hire someone to run the branch in Virginia and start one here.

It seemed that I got everything I wanted. A family of my own.

Micah enjoyed that I had taken my eyes off of her and started seeing Jermel. After he stepped to me like a man about her, I wasn't too much tripping about it. He knew that I would peel his top back blue if he so much as looked at her wrong.

"I love that, shit," I commented and pulled her by the waist into my body gently.

"Stop it," she giggled girlishly. "You know I don't care about all of that. I just want to be at peace with you and our baby, that's it."

"I know, it's one of them thangs that I really love about you," I shared, molding my hands against her spreading hips.

She looked up like she didn't know a nigga loved her ass. "Stop it, Dre."

"Stop what? I ain't playin'. You think you got knocked up cause I'm reckless? All that shit was on purpose."

She huffed and smacked her lips. "Yeah, you got some nerve too."

"I wasn't about to be one of your old nigga's standing on the sidelines with a wish I shoulda, coulda, woulda because you were off happy with someone else. I had to make sure that those seven days went on for life."

"I can't stand you," she groaned. "You could've just told me. You didn't have to knock me up."

"Ay, don't act like it wasn't worth it." I caressed her cheek and watched that pretty ass smile creep across her face.

"Every second," she replied softly. "Tell me what else you love."

"You." One kiss to her cheek. "All of you." Another to her supple lips.

"I'm intentional about your love. I'm crazy about that shit. I don't want to live without it." The final kiss to her belly. "That's us. Love, in human form. Impulsive emotion, intentional bomb ass love."

Kendra's soft palm ran over my waves then down my face. "Keep that same energy when it's two am and the baby is hungry and needs to be changed. Aight, lil daddy?"

"Yeah, I'm sure you will."

I chuckled as she drew back her hands and kissed her teeth. "You work my damn nerves."

She turned around and started back to the house. "But you love me."

"Eh, let's see how much I love you in five months when I have to push this giant out."

The thought of it made me wince. "And I'm gon' to support that. From right here!"

She waved me off and continued to walk away. I stood there in awe of everything she was. And everything she was, was mine too. I loved that woman. I knew from the moment I looked at her.

The End

AFTERWORD

Thank you so much for reading! This was so much fun to write. I want to give a quick shout out to my BLP sisters and my actual sisters for pushing me to the finish line. I hope you enjoyed DeAndre and Kendra in this naughty novella. Please leave a review, join my mailing list and group for exclusive content.

See you between the pages!

TMC

- A.P.

ALSO BY AUBREE PYNN

Thank you for reading! Make sure you check out my catalog:

URBAN ROMANCE

Dope Boys

Her Goon, His Eden

Run From Me

contemporary romance

Everything is love

My Love For You: The Collection

Love 101

Color Me, You

Because Love Said So

Say He'll Be My Valentine

Get Me Back

Impulsive Emotion

The Last Christmas

Concourse D with Love

Edible Arrangements

Completed Series

The Way you Lie 1-2

All to Myself 1-2

Love the Series 1-4

Indigo Haze 1-4

Forbidden lust series 1-4

one last chance 1-3 (COLLAB)

POETRY COLLECTION

COLDEST SUMMER EVER

SUMWHEREOVARAINBOWS

QUEENDOM

THE ESSENCE OF YOU

STRANGER THINGS: A COLLECTION OF
UNMASTERED EMOTION

Connect with me on my social media:

IG: @aubreepynn

TWITTER: @aubreepynn

Facebook: Aubreé Pynn

Check out my website:

Aubreepynnwrites.wordpress.com

A million words, in a million books, is never thank you enough for your support.